SOUTH POLE SANTA
SANTA
THE LEGEND OF NICNOTT

WRITTEN BY THE GAUDIOSO TWINS

This children's book is dedicated to
our loving mother, Maryann and the imagination she inspired in us.

Santa put on his best sleeping cap.
He slid on his slippers, and tucked in the cat.

Mrs. Claus stoked the chimney, 4 times like before
then stubbed her small toe on a nail in the floor.

"Ouch" she exclaimed as she climbed into bed,
but Santa was sleeping, sweet dreams in his head.

She waved to the reindeer wishing them goodnight,
since they were now tired from their round-the-world flight.
And with that she let from her small hands release,
Santa's long naughty list and his signed decree.

It flew into the night and
Mrs. Claus called out.
"Not bad considering
all the children throughout,
the world and its lights,
its noise, and its clutter."
Now Mrs. Claus was cold
so she drew in the shutters.

NAUGHTY LIST

The shutters shook.
Oh, the shutters did shake
then outside the window
a luster took shape.
It coiled to the left
and coiled to the right

Then all in an instant
it flew out of sight.
It flew to the north,
then it flew to the south
but not before passing
the Unca Too Too's house.

This white mythical creature
is still shrouded in doubt,
but it felt the cold of the luster
and it started to shout.

The Unca stomped up.
The Unca stomped down.
The Unca turned sideways
then ran all around.

The Unca shook its fists
then dove in the snow.
This Unca scares easy!
Oh, didn't you know?

It took the NAUGHTY LIST down to the South Pole, where few ever visit, where less ever go.

There lives a man
that time forgot,
It's South Pole Santa,
better known as Nicnott.
Stingy and cold
from his head to his toes,
Nicnott is constantly
blowing his nose.

He marches about
and stomps his feet,
He curses the weather.
He curses the sleet.
His only friend is that of Jack Frost
and without that nymph
he'd be totally lost.

Now on this Christmas, the meter did sound
and Nicnott livened and spun around.
For a 4 on the meter certainly implied,
at least some of the children in the world
had been naughty, not nice.

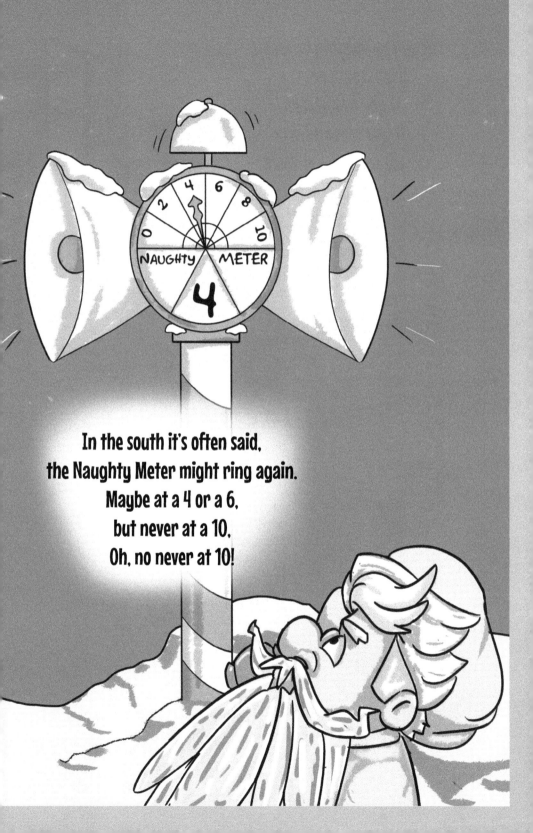

In the south it's often said,
the Naughty Meter might ring again.
Maybe at a 4 or a 6,
but never at a 10,
Oh, no never at 10!

If you're naughty or mean,
if you tease or cuss,
if you misbehave,
if you cause a fuss,
if you scream and shout
and run amok,
then on Christmas Eve,
you're out of luck.

Through the ice Nicnott skates,
not a second too long,
not a second to waste.
With Jack Frost skiing by his side,
Nicnott keeps a watchful eye,

and through your window Nicnott slides
to place his coal at your bedside.
He snickers and sneers and celebrates,
then eats Santa's last cookie,
and even the plate!

So, if on this Christmas
you don't wish for socks
and if on this Christmas
you don't want coal rocks,

do all of your studies, to others be kind.
Santa likes NICE names, shining so bright...
MERRY CHRISTMAS TO ALL AND TO ALL A GOODNIGHT!!

SIGN YOUR NAME TO SANTA'S NICE LIST AS SOON AS POSSIBLE.

_____

_____

_____

_____

_____

_____

_____

_____

_____

_____

CPSIA information can be obtained
at www.ICGtesting.com
Printed in the USA
BVHW091041030222
627978BV00002B/110